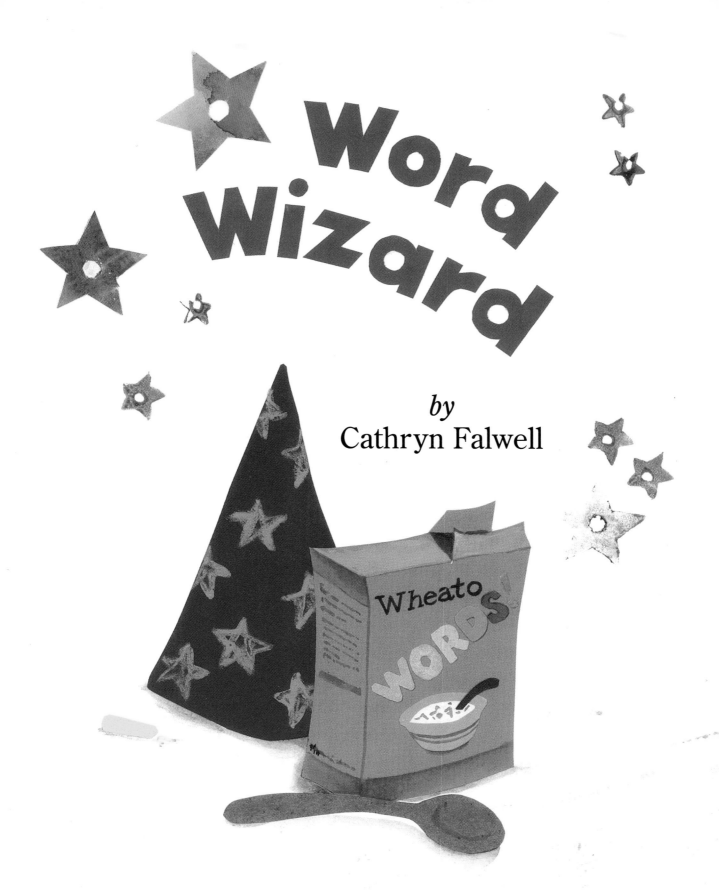

Word Wizard

by
Cathryn Falwell

Clarion Books / *New York*

Clarion Books
a Houghton Mifflin Company imprint
215 Park Avenue South, New York, NY 10003
Text and illustrations copyright © 1998 by Cathryn Falwell

The illustrations were executed in cut paper collage, rubber stamp prints,
and watercolors
The text was set in 17/23-point Century Old Style

Printed in the USA

Library of Congress Cataloging-in-Publication Data
Falwell, Cathryn.
Word wizard / by Cathryn Falwell.
p.   cm.
Summary: Using her magical spoon to make new words by changing letters around,
Anna embarks on a series of adventures with a lost little boy.
ISBN: 0-395-85580-2
[1. English language—Spelling—Fiction. 2. Imagination—Fiction.] I. Title.
PZ7.F19Wo   1998
[E]—dc21
97-17710
CIP
AC

HOR 10 9 8 7 6 5 4 3 2 1

In memory
of my wonderful mother,
Leona Chauvin Falwell
who loved words

Early one morning,
Anna was eating
breakfast.
She dipped her spoon
into the bowl.
The cereal letters
spelled

Anna watched
the letters float
around in the spoon.
Now they spelled

"Magic!" said Anna,
finishing her breakfast.

6

And
with
the
magic
spoon
for a
wand,
Anna
became
a

Word
wizard!

PAT
TAP

gum

flea
leaf

mug

STAR
ARTS

Anna began to change all kinds of words.
A small sad boy appeared next to her.
"Hi. I'm Anna," she told him,
"and I'm a WORD WIZARD!"
"I'm Zack," said the boy,
"and I'm LOST!"
"I'll help you," said Anna.

9

With a wave
of her wand, Zack's

tears

. . . along with

the **m** that had
lingered
in her spoon . . .

a t s e m o c

. . . changed into a gentle

stream

The stream flowed into a
wave-tossed ocean.
"This won't do," said Anna,
and she rearranged

OCEAN

into

CANOE

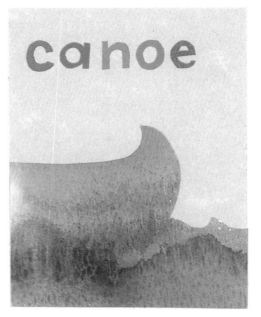

Then she and Zack
paddled peacefully
to shore.

A quick wave
of her spoon
turned

shore

into

horse.

"I'm tired and hungry," cried Zack, following in Anna's tracks. "Watch!" said Anna, as she changed

track

into

cart.

She gave Zack the leftover

k

to munch on.

16

17

Suddenly, a beast appeared!
Zack's sword was no match.

Anna grabbed the **k**
just in time, and turned

BEAST

into

BA**S**K**ET**

"That was close,"
said Anna.
Away they rode.

But the road was blocked
by a large stone.

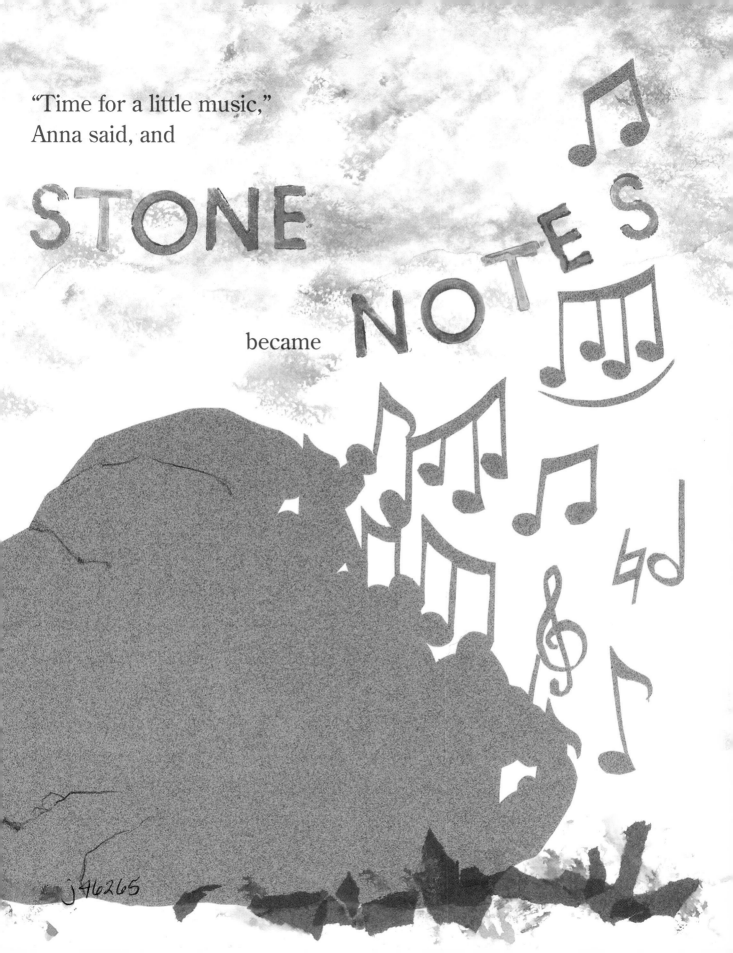

"Time for a little music," Anna said, and

STONE

became NOTES

They began to sing along
with the music. With Zack's
help, Anna changed

sing to **Wings**

and away they flew.
"I'm still hungry," said Zack.
Sour lemons grew below.

So of course,
Anna changed

lemons

into

melons

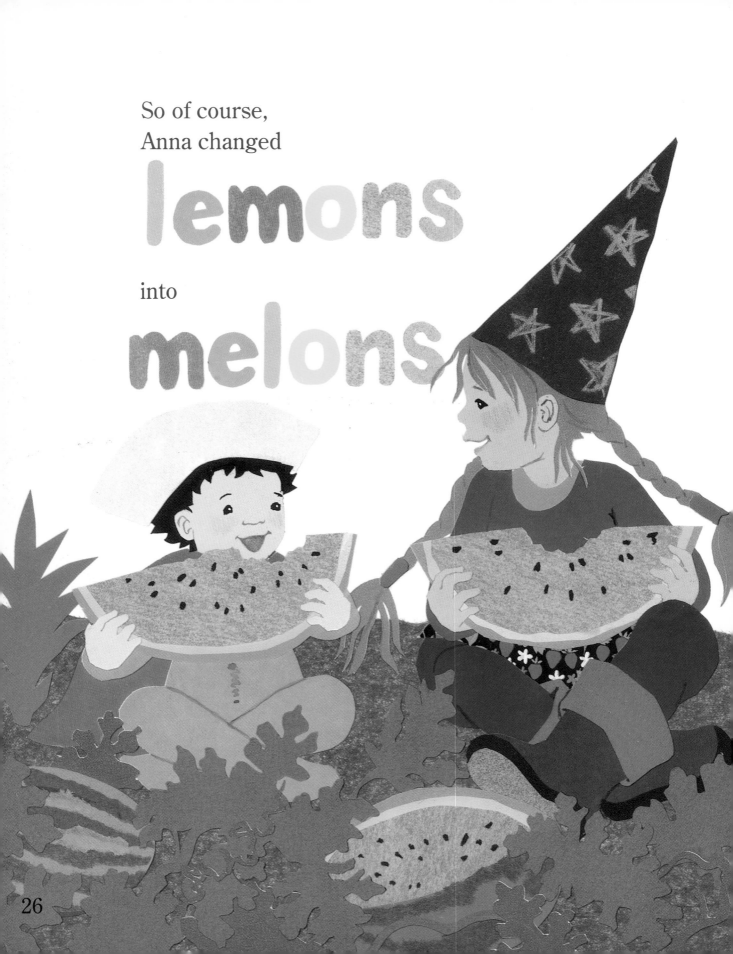

"Yum!" said Zack,
wiping juice from his chin.
He looked around.
"I'M HOME!"

28

"Good-bye, Zack,"
said Anna.

"But wait!" cried Zack.
"What if I get lost again?"

"You'll be able to help
yourself," said Anna.

She waved her wand
and changed Zack's

sword...

. . . into **words**

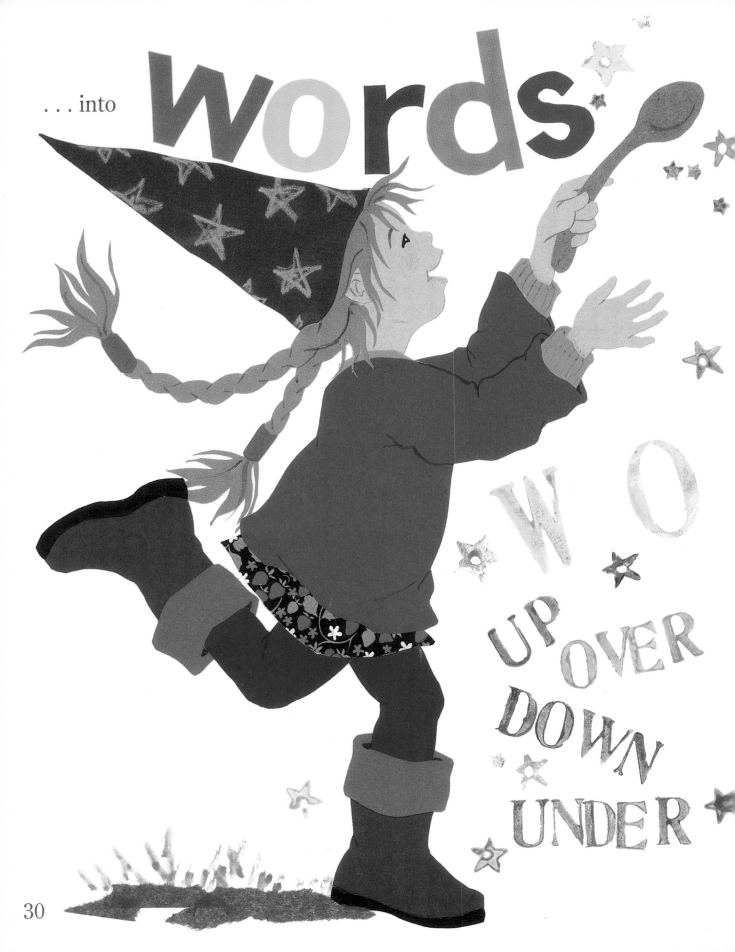

W O
UP OVER
DOWN
UNDER

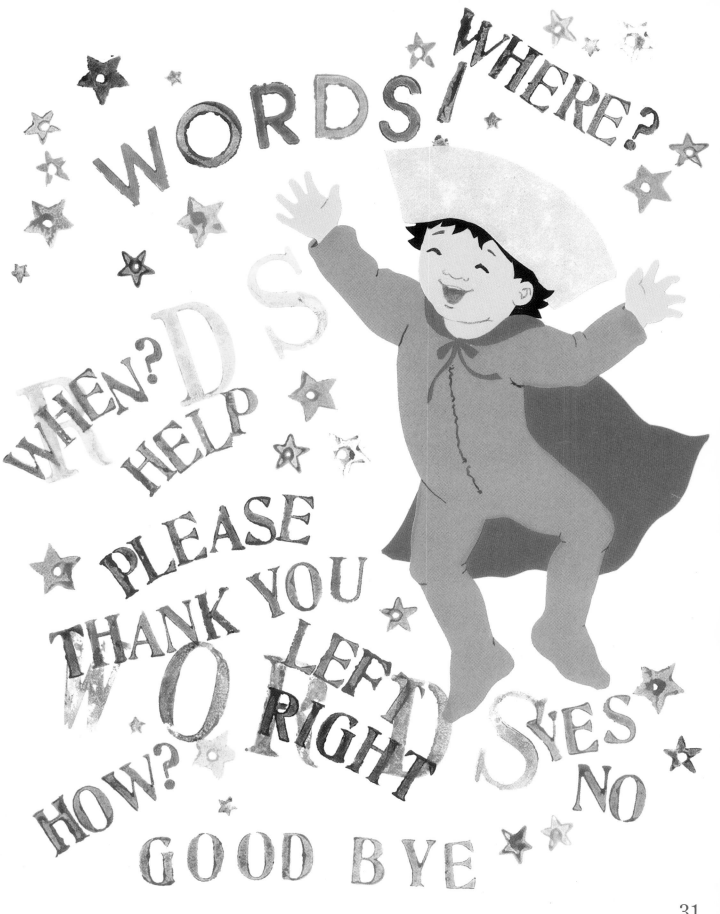

WORDS! WHERE? WHEN? HELP PLEASE THANK YOU LEFT RIGHT YES NO HOW? GOOD BYE

You Can Be a
Word Wizard!

When Anna scrambles the letters of a word to create a new word, she is making an *anagram*: a word or phrase formed by reordering the letters of another word or phrase.

A set of moveable letters makes anagrams fun to try. You may already have alphabet blocks or magnetic letters. Here are other ideas:

 Collect letters from cereal boxes and other cartons.

Cut large letters from magazines, newspapers, and mail advertisements. Glue them to squares of cardboard or heavy paper.

Look for alphabet pasta at your local health food store. Then you can eat your words.

Be creative! You can make letters from all kinds of things.

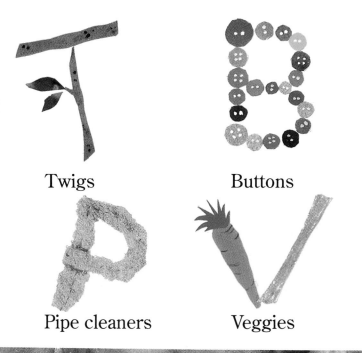

Twigs   Buttons

Pipe cleaners   Veggies

The pictures for *Word Wizard* are made from cut paper collage (Ko-LAZH). Lots of different kinds of paper scraps were cut and pasted onto heavy white paper. You might enjoy making collages, too. Start collecting scraps—pieces of old gift wrap, envelopes, labels—anything! Anna's magic spoon was cut from a grocery sack! Have fun!